Butterflies

FOR

GRANDPA

JOE

3/22

Butterflies
FOR
GRANDPA
JOE

NICOLA DAVIES

ILLUSTRATED BY
MIKE BYRNE

Barrington Stoke

First published in 2019 in Great Britain by
Barrington Stoke Ltd
18 Walker Street, Edinburgh, EH3 7LP

www.barringtonstoke.co.uk

Text © 2019 Nicola Davies
Illustrations © 2019 Mike Byrne

The moral right of Nicola Davies and Mike Byrne to be identified
as the author and illustrator of this work has been asserted in
accordance with the Copyright, Designs and Patents Act, 1988

A CIP catalogue record for this book is available
from the British Library upon request

ISBN: 978-1-78112-882-4

Printed in China by Leo

For Joanna, this one's just for you

Contents

CHAPTER 1

CAKES AND BUTTERFLIES

Ben loved his granny and grandpa's garden.
It was nothing like his own garden at home.
That was not a proper garden at all, just a
square covered in concrete. But in Granny
Lou and Grandpa Joe's garden, the flowers
bloomed in higgledy-piggledy beds, the grass
grew tall and weedy, and it was always full of
bees, butterflies and birds.

"It's our private jungle!" Granny Lou would say, and Grandpa Joe would shake his butterfly net and laugh. "And *I'm* going on safari!"

Granny Lou would grin and say, "Butterfly mad, he is! Totally butterfly bonkers!"

*

Today, when Ben pushed open the gate at the side of his grandparents' house, everything looked so different. The garden felt grey and sad after a long winter. It was as if it knew that Granny was gone and Grandpa hadn't been outside for months. Ben sighed as he took the spare back-door key from behind a loose brick in the wall.

That was where Granny Lou had always hidden the key. "Shhh," she used to say with a wink. "Don't tell your grandpa! He says the burglars will get in."

Ben was the only person left who knew about Granny's secret key. He unlocked the door, put the key back behind the brick and went inside.

The house was dark and still. The only clue that anyone lived here was the blue flicker of the TV from the living room.

Ben took off his coat and went through to see Grandpa. He was sitting on the sofa, staring at the TV screen with the sound turned off. He'd done that all day, every day since Granny Lou's funeral.

"Hi, Grandpa Joe!" Ben said. "Had a good day?"

Slowly Grandpa Joe turned to look at his grandson. His face was pale and distant, like a moon reflected in a puddle.

"Yes," he said softly. "Yes, thanks." Then he turned back to the telly and said no more.

"I'll get your tea," Ben said.

The kitchen seemed too tidy now. When Granny Lou was alive, there were bowls and cake tins everywhere. Granny Lou made lots and lots of cakes. Her cakes were famous – she made them for anyone who wanted one.

"Never for money, always for love!" she told Ben.

Ben had spent winter weekends helping her bake cakes for as long as he could remember. They had made pink sponge dinosaurs, castles made of chocolate brownies and, once, a fruit cake that Granny iced so it looked like a garden.

Grandpa Joe had always left them in peace, because he'd be in his shed, sorting the thousands of photos of butterflies he'd taken and planning the new photographs he wanted to take when it was summer again.

As soon as spring came, Granny Lou and Grandpa Joe would be outside in their garden all day long. No matter how early Ben arrived on a Saturday morning, there they'd be: Granny with her sun hat and gardening

gloves, and Grandpa fiddling with his camera
and tripod so as to get a perfect shot of one
of the butterflies that fluttered about over
the flowers.

Sometimes, Grandpa would go off on
an "expedition" and vanish in his rusty old
car so he could photograph other kinds of
butterfly that never came to the garden.

Ben didn't know what the other
butterflies looked like, but he loved to hear
their weird names – Swallowtails, Adonis
Blues, Large Coppers.

Sometimes, Granny and Ben would go
with Grandpa and eat a picnic in a field or a
wood while he chased about with his net and
his camera.

At the end of every Saturday they would eat together – sometimes their supper was just cake. That was another secret Ben had promised to keep! Then they would play cards.

Grandpa never took the games seriously and would try to cheat in silly ways, hiding cards up his sleeve or in his pocket. He made Ben and Granny Lou laugh so much that Ben often went to bed still giggling.

All that was like another world now. Ben made some cheese sandwiches and tea for Grandpa Joe, then slid the tray onto the table next to Grandpa and sat down on the sofa beside him.

He looked around the room at the photos of sunlit butterflies that were all over the walls. Was it really Grandpa Joe who had taken all those photos? It was hard to remember that the person who had taken them was the same old man who now sat chewing his sandwiches without looking away from the TV or saying a word.

*

Ben stayed with his grandfather until Mrs Johns, Grandpa Joe's night-time carer, came.

"Bye, Grandpa," Ben said. "Maybe next time I come we could go in the garden? Won't be long till spring now!"

9

Grandpa looked up, but he didn't seem to see Ben at all. He shook his head slowly. When he said, "Not outside, thanks", his voice sounded as if it was coming from far, far away. Then he turned back to the TV.

He's slipping away! Ben thought with a sudden stab of panic. *I'm losing him.*

As Ben sat on the bus on the way home, he stared out at the dark streets and thought about what he could do to bring Grandpa Joe back to life.

CHAPTER 2

AN IDEA HATCHES

When he got home, Ben's head was full of ideas about Grandpa Joe and what to do, but everything was in a muddle.

He wanted to talk to Mum about his ideas; she was good at sorting out muddles. But it was difficult to talk to Mum these days. She was always so busy with her job as a teacher as well as looking after Ben's little twin sisters.

And talking to Mum about Grandpa was always extra difficult. Something had gone wrong between her and his grandparents. Ben didn't understand why.

Ben's dad was called Stewart. He was Grandpa and Granny's only son. He had died from a heart attack with no warning when he was just 43. Ben was still very small then; he didn't remember Stewart at all.

After his dad had died, Mum and Ben had lived with Grandpa and Granny for a long time. Ben remembered those years. He'd been really happy: afternoons after school pottering around with Granny and Grandpa, evenings reading stories with his mum.

Everything changed when Mum met Keith, Ben's stepdad. Ben liked Keith from the start. He was kind and easy-going, and he had a really cool accent because he was from America.

Granny Lou and Grandpa Joe seemed to like Keith too at first. But after Mum and Keith got married, things weren't the same. Mum, Keith and Ben moved to a new house across town. Then the twins were born and they stopped seeing Granny and Grandpa.

Ben wasn't sure what had happened. Maybe Granny Lou and Mum had fallen out; maybe they had an argument. Ben didn't know. All he knew was that Granny and Grandpa stopped visiting, and Mum didn't even talk about it.

Ben missed Granny and Grandpa so much, and as soon as he was old enough he began to spend most weekends at their house. That was OK with Mum and Keith. In fact, sometimes Ben thought that they were glad when he went away on Saturday mornings.

But now Ben *had* to talk to Mum about Grandpa Joe. After all, he and Mum were Joe's only family.

While Keith was giving the twins their bath, Ben went into the kitchen to talk to

Mum as she made supper. He started to tell her how worried he was.

"Grandpa Joe's still not going out," he began.

"Hmmm," said Mum. Ben knew she wasn't really paying attention.

"Mum!" Ben began again. "Please listen."

"What? Oh, sorry, love." She smiled over the top of her glasses. "I'm listening now."

"Grandpa Joe—" Ben began again.

"You are the best grandson," Mum said. "You go there every day. You really don't have to. He's got Mrs Johns."

"I don't do it to be a good grandson," Ben
replied. "I want to help Grandpa Joe. He
just sits on the sofa *all day*. It's like he's not
himself any more. And I miss him."

Mum stopped what she was doing and put
her arm round Ben.

"Something broke in him when Lou died," she said with a sigh. "I don't think it's ever going to mend."

Keith came downstairs just then and he stood at the kitchen door as Ben and Mum were talking.

"Poor old Grandpa Joe, eh?" Keith said sadly. "I think your mom is right, Ben. Actually, we have been thinking a lot about Grandpa Joe."

Keith and Mum gave each other a look that Ben didn't understand, and then there was a smell of burning and suddenly everyone was busy again.

"Can we talk about Joe another time, love?" Mum said. "I've just got to rescue dinner!"

"Sure." Keith gave a shrug, then he turned to Ben and said, "Your sisters *badly* need their big bro to read them a story!"

What did that look between Mum and Keith mean? Ben couldn't help feeling that there was something they weren't telling him about Grandpa Joe. But his little sisters were waiting for him, and there was no time to think about it any more.

His little sisters were called Beedee and Deebee. Their real names were Beatrice and Daphne, but they had called themselves

Beedee and Deebee as soon as they could talk. They were three.

It was hard to read stories to the girls because they interrupted all the time. This evening they were so chatty that Ben gave up altogether and flopped on one bed while the girls bounced up and down on the other. They talked fast and in an odd way. People outside the family never understood them.

"Wewent'see butflieswivnurseree," said Deebee. She ran all her words together, but Ben knew what she meant: "We went to see butterflies with nursery."

"Yes!" Beedee added. "It was very 'mazing!"

The girls rolled around in giggles, and Ben found himself giggling too. When they had all stopped, the girls sat side by side to tell him about another special part of their day.

"The poticalbutfly house," Deebee said. *Potical?* It took Ben a moment to work that one out.

"Oh, tropical butterfly house!" he said.

Beedee nodded. "Potical. S'what she said."

"It was hot," Deebee said, "and we got butflies on our hands."

"Real live ones!" Beedee said. "They had nantstennies and lickle feets."

Antennae and little feet, Ben understood in his head.

"And," Deebee added, "we saw one being born!"

Ben was pretty sure butterflies weren't "born", but he didn't say anything. The girls were chatting about the butterflies' bright colours and their fluttering wings. He had never seen them so excited about anything.

Deebee and Beedee were still talking about the "butflies" when they fell asleep at last, flopped together on one bed. Ben put the duvet over them.

They were so cute and funny; he adored them. But their excited talk about the butterflies "being born" and walking all over their hands had also given him an

idea. If Grandpa wouldn't leave his sofa to
go outside, then perhaps Ben could bring
butterflies to Grandpa and bring him back to
life and to the safaris in his garden!

CHAPTER 3

THE FIRST BUTTERFLY OF SPRING

The next day was Saturday. When Granny Lou was alive, Ben would head off for the weekend at his grandparents' house first thing on Saturday. But Mrs Johns was there on Saturday mornings now. She cleaned, tidied up and did the washing. Ben didn't want to be in the way. And he knew he'd get fed up sitting indoors with Grandpa all day long.

So instead, he lay in bed and listened to
Keith pretending to be a bear and chasing
the twins up and down the landing, and to
Mum singing out of tune in the shower.

He didn't really feel part of weekends at
home any more. What would it have been
like if Stewart hadn't died? Would Ben have
different little sisters now, or no sisters at
all? And he couldn't imagine what life would
be like without Keith there. Ben's thoughts
got in a muddle again, so he went back to
sleep.

When he woke, everything was quiet.
Keith had taken the twins swimming; Mum
had gone shopping. He was alone in an

empty house, thinking of Grandpa on his sofa.

He went downstairs and stood in the kitchen in his PJs, eating cereal straight from the packet.

There was a knock at the door. His friend Matt stood on the doorstep with a football under his arm. When he saw Ben, he beamed, like the sun coming out from behind a cloud.

"Didn't think you'd be in!" Matt said. "Fancy a kick-about in the park?"

Ben beamed back. It was so good to see his best friend! And it had been ages since they'd played football together.

"Brilliant! I'll get my kit on." Ben ran up the stairs two at a time.

It was grey and cold, but the boys soon warmed up, skidding in the mud to score and diving for saves. They pretended they were scoring the winning goals for their favourite teams or saving penalties in the World Cup.

For two whole hours, Ben forgot all about Grandpa Joe. Then the sun came out – spring was on its way. Every spring, Grandpa started to get ready for the butterfly expeditions that warmer days would bring. Ben and Matt sat on a bench for a breather, and Ben told his friend about his plan to bring butterflies to Grandpa Joe.

"The problem is," Ben explained, "that I spent more time making cakes with Granny Lou. I don't know much about Grandpa Joe's butterflies."

Matt laughed. "A pink sponge dinosaur isn't going to be much help now," he said.

"I mean, I know that caterpillars turn into butterflies," Ben said, "but how, and how long does it take? And where do you get caterpillars from?"

"No idea!" Matt said. "But isn't that what the internet is for?"

"Yeah, I suppose," said Ben. "I just don't know where to start."

Matt gave a shout of surprise and pointed over Ben's shoulder. "There! That's where you start! Perhaps you could just catch one?"

Ben spun round just in time to see a butterfly the colour of lemon juice vanish over the wall of the park. It was as if Grandpa Joe had said something right in his ear: *Look, Ben! First butterfly of spring! What a beauty!*

"What was that?" Ben gasped.

Matt looked at him as if he was stupid. "A butterfly, you idiot!"

Ben started to tell Matt that there were different *kinds* of butterfly (*See, I know that much, Grandpa*, he told Joe in his head), but Matt had a brain full of football. He was never going to get it. But perhaps he was right about the lemon-yellow butterfly being the start ...

Back at the house, after Matt had gone home, Ben got his laptop and typed in "first butterfly of spring, yellow".

He found a picture of the butterfly they had seen in the park! It was called a Brimstone. (Grandpa's voice said, *Remember – I taught you that already, Ben?*)

It had hibernated all through the winter! Ben was amazed. How could that tiny, fragile creature survive for all that time? Where did it hide?

He found out about Brimstone eggs and caterpillars (*Who knew they only ate one kind of leaf?* Ben thought) and how they changed into butterflies with wings, eyes and long legs, inside a chrysalis.

It took at least two weeks for a butterfly to emerge from its chrysalis, but a whole month or more before that for the caterpillars to grow big enough to build the chrysalis in the first place.

That meant Ben's plan would take at least six weeks to work. And that was if he knew where to find butterfly eggs or caterpillars. Six more weeks of Grandpa sitting on that sofa all day, every day.

Ben felt like giving up, then he clicked on a link that said "How to look after butterflies and moths". That led him to exactly what he needed: a website called Butterfly Bonanza where you could buy caterpillars, and which told you how to care for them so they would grow and turn into butterflies. Ben could hardly believe it! It sold everything he would need.

There were different kinds of butterfly to choose from. Some were huge and very bright, like the ones the girls had seen at the zoo. But these came from far-away tropical countries, and Ben was pretty sure Grandpa had only ever been interested in British butterflies. Ben thought it would be best to stick with butterflies that Grandpa had seen and photographed many times. Besides, Ben had never kept caterpillars before, so he would need something easy to look after and which didn't need a hot greenhouse to live in!

The website said that Painted Lady butterflies were the easiest to rear. Ben remembered seeing them in Granny Lou's garden and in Grandpa's photos. They were about the size of a credit card, with lovely orange, white and black patterns on their wings.

Ben ran upstairs and tipped the money out of the jam jar where he kept his savings. There was just enough to pay for the caterpillars and a mesh cage to keep them in!

But when he told Mum and Keith about his plan after the girls had gone to bed, they gave each other that strange look again.

"Your butterfly idea is great," said Keith. "But don't get your hopes up too much about Grandpa."

"The thing is, love," Mum said, "we've had to make a very hard decision about Grandpa Joe."

"Mrs Johns says he's getting worse," Keith added, "and that he needs full-time care."

"He doesn't!" Ben cried. "He just needs to stop sitting on the sofa!"

"Ben, we have to keep Grandpa Joe safe, because he's not able to take care of himself any more and we're his only family," Keith said softly. "So we're going to sell his house and use the money to pay for a care home for him."

"Grandpa Joe wouldn't want to sell his home!" Ben cried. "He'd hate to live in a care home!"

"I think he'd want to do what's best for his health and safety," Mum said with a sigh.

Ben couldn't believe what he was hearing. "What do either of you know about what he'd want?" he shouted. "You never visit him. Even when Granny Lou was alive you didn't visit. You never even asked him to come and stay here when she died!"

"Ben, that's not fair." Mum was beginning to sound cross, so Keith put up his hand to try to keep the peace.

"Hey, everybody. Let's just cool it here."

"I'm sorry," said Mum. "I don't want to fall out with you about this, Ben," she said. "We do care about Joe."

"Yes," Keith added, "we care very much, Ben. But it's not easy. Grandma Lou said some hard things when your mom and I got together. She was still sad about Stewart, I guess. But it made things difficult between us."

"Lou didn't like me marrying Keith. She didn't want to see the girls, and Grandpa Joe just went along with it all," Mum said. "When Granny Lou died, we did ask Grandpa Joe to come here, but he wouldn't." Mum sounded really sad now.

"Why didn't you tell me all this before?" Ben asked.

"We didn't want to make you feel bad about Lou," Keith said, "or Joe – you loved them so much."

Mum shook her head slowly.

"It's too late to make things better now, with Joe the way he is," she said. "He's never going to get better."

Ben felt torn in two. The problems in his family were serious. He ran upstairs to his bedroom and lay down, staring into the dark.

As he did, he began to think of tiny eggs that hatched into caterpillars, just simple little sacs of life that could change, so totally, into butterflies. It *was* amazing. And suddenly he felt better. Mum just might be wrong. Change just might be possible.

Ben sat up and switched on the light. He got a pen and paper and wrote a letter to Butterfly Bonanza to order all he needed for his Painted Lady plan. He put it in an envelope with the money to pay for everything. He would post it on the way to school in the morning.

Maybe it wasn't too late for Joe and for the healing that this family needed. It certainly wasn't too late to try.

CHAPTER 4

GROW, GROW, GROW

When Ben got to Grandpa Joe's after school that Thursday, an estate agent was putting up a For Sale sign in the front garden. Ben scowled at him and went round to the back and into the garden. When the caterpillars arrived, they would need nettles to eat. Granny Lou had always let the nettles grow at the bottom of the garden.

Ben got a spade, three empty pots from the shed and Granny's old gardening gloves. The nettles were already sprouting now that it was almost spring, and their small leaves were super stingy. But it was worth it.

He planted clumps in each of the pots, then put them into a box to carry home on the bus.

Inside the house, Grandpa Joe was on the sofa as always. He was looking even more pale and thin and even more lost than last week.

As the old man chewed his way through his sandwich and sipped his tea, he looked almost like a ghost, just a husk of the person

43

that Grandpa Joe used to be. But Ben was not going to give up. He was determined now.

Ben looked at all the butterfly photos on the wall. He found a really good one of what he was almost sure was a Painted Lady. He took it down and went to sit next to his grandpa on the sofa. Then he turned on all the lights in the room and turned off the TV.

At first the old man kept staring at the dark screen, then he looked at Ben with a puzzled face.

"Why d'you turn it off?"

Ben was so happy! At least Grandpa Joe had noticed something for a change!

"Cos I want you to look at something, Grandpa Joe," Ben said. "Here!"

Ben laid the bright photo on his grandpa's lap.

"Remember this?" he asked. "It's a Painted Lady, isn't it?"

Grandpa looked at the photo, then back at Ben, his face once more blank as a sheet of paper. But Ben went on, "I'm going to rear some caterpillars of these and bring the butterflies right into this room! So they will sit on your hand. What do you think of that?"

Grandpa turned his face back to the blank TV screen.

"Turn it on," he said softly. Then, more loudly, "Turn it *on*!"

"No!" Ben replied. "I *won't* turn it on."

Suddenly Ben felt cross. Not just cross, bursting. Words that he hadn't planned to say came spurting out, hot as blood.

"Why was Granny Lou horrid about Keith and Mum? Why didn't you say something? Why don't you want to see my little sisters? And why didn't you ever talk to me about my dad?"

There was a long silence. When at last Grandpa Joe turned to look at Ben, he was frowning. He tapped the photo with one angry finger.

"Small Tortoiseshell!" he said. "Not a
Painted Lady."

Ben looked at the photo. Grandpa was
right: it wasn't a Painted Lady. This butterfly

had a little row of blue dots around its wings. Painted Ladies never had that.

"It's not a Painted Lady!" Grandpa said again, then he reached over to the remote control and switched the TV on for himself!

The front door opened and Mrs Johns called out "Hello!" The hot anger had gone now, and Ben was laughing to himself. It was just like Grandpa Joe to get crosser about a butterfly with the wrong name than about being asked personal questions. So like the *old* Grandpa Joe, who cheated at cards and went on safari in the garden.

Ben felt so hopeful that he ignored the funny looks he got from people on the bus because of his big box of nettles.

Back home, the parcel from Butterfly Bonanza had already arrived – that felt like another good sign.

Ben put the first pot of nettles in the middle of his bedroom windowsill. Then he put the mesh cage around it and hooked the top of the cage to the curtain rod.

He'd told Beedee and Deebee they could watch if they sat still on the bed, but as Ben opened the little box with the caterpillars inside, they got up to see them. The caterpillars were very small, like tiny maggots with a coat of black spiky hair.

"They're sooo teeny!" Deebee said.

"And hairy!" Beedee added. "Will they really be butflies?"

Ben told them that, yes, of course they would. But the creatures seemed so small, so totally different from anything with pretty orange wings, that he wasn't sure he believed it himself.

Very carefully, he put the caterpillars onto the nettles. Could you tell if they were happy or hungry? Ben didn't know. All he could do was tuck the netting cage around everything so the caterpillars were safe inside and keep his fingers crossed.

By the next morning, there were holes in some of the nettle leaves! The caterpillars were eating!

Two days later the nettles looked like
green lace – more holes than leaf. The
floor of the mesh cage was covered in tiny
green poos. The twins thought that was
the funniest thing they had ever seen. Ben
cleaned them away and put in fresh nettles.

After a few days, the caterpillars were much bigger. And not just bigger – they were prettier too, with little dots of red and green on their black skins. Still, it was hard to believe they would ever be butterflies.

Ben sat with the girls and together they watched the caterpillars wiggle about on the leaves, eating, eating, eating.

"Their moufs is sideways," Beedee said.

Ben laughed. She was right! The little creatures munched through the nettles by chewing side to side, not up and down like other animals.

"Why don't they get stung?" Deebee asked.

Ben shook his head; he had no idea.

"I'll ask Grandpa Joe when he's better," he said.

*

It was all going well, then suddenly the caterpillars stopped eating. Ben panicked. Were they going to die? What had he done wrong? He came straight home after school so he could look at the Butterfly Bonanza website.

"When the caterpillars stop eating," Ben read, "it means they're ready to shed their skins. It's a good sign. They're growing."

Ben watched carefully. It was just as the website said. The next day the caterpillars were eating again, and he could see the tiny dried-up skins they had shed hanging on the half-eaten leaves.

*

Most days after school, Ben went over to visit Grandpa Joe. Each time, he switched off the telly and told Grandpa Joe all about the caterpillars.

Grandpa didn't say anything, but Ben could see he was listening, *really* listening. But even as the weather got warmer, Grandpa Joe would not move from his sofa. When Ben asked if he'd like a walk around the garden, or got Grandpa's camera out and put it on his lap, he just shook his head.

It'll all change when he sees the butterflies, Ben told himself. *I know it will!*

Ben could tell that Mum and Keith didn't think his plan was going to work, but they were nice about the caterpillars and did come and look at them.

"Wow. They must be twenty times bigger than they were!" Keith said one evening as he looked into their mesh cage.

Ben nodded. "They're almost ready to pupate."

"Then how long does it take for them to turn into butterflies?" Mum asked.

"About twelve days," Ben told her.

"So in two weeks they could be flying!" Keith said.

"The caterpillars need to grow a bit more before they're big enough to make their chrysalises," Ben said. "So I think it could be nearer to three weeks."

Keith and Mum did "the look" at each other.

"Somebody wants to buy Joe's house, Ben," Mum said. "They want to sign the contracts by Easter."

Ben didn't reply. Easter was in seventeen days – that was less than three weeks away. Perhaps the butterflies could still make it. Grandpa could get off the sofa, be his old self and walk back into his garden, his house and his life. Silently, Ben willed the caterpillars to grow, grow, grow.

CHAPTER 5

IT'S NEVER TOO LATE

The caterpillars did grow! Just five days after Ben and his mum and Keith were watching them, ten perfect little chrysalises were dotted about the mesh cage!

But there were just twelve days left before Grandpa Joe's house would be sold to a new owner, and Grandpa had to move out. Ben felt that once Grandpa was living

somewhere new, it would be too late for the old Grandpa Joe to come back.

The Easter holidays began, and Ben tried not to spend too long staring at the still, silent little chrysalises. He went to the park with Matt. Played with the twins. Walked about in Grandpa's garden, where the flowers were beginning to wake up. All the time he felt the hours and days ticking away.

Ten days; eight days; five; three.

On the Thursday before Easter, Mum knocked on his bedroom door.

"Can I come in?" she said.

Ben sat up in bed and smiled.

"Today's the day, Ben," Mum said. "It looks like the contract for the sale of Grandpa's house will be signed today."

Ben was puzzled. "What does that mean?" he asked.

"When the contract is signed, that means the house is sold by law," Mum explained.

"But you said by Easter!" Ben cried. "I thought we had three more days!"

"I didn't explain properly. Today is the last *working* day before Easter. That was the deadline."

"Couldn't it wait just one more day?" Ben pleaded. "I'm sure they'll emerge today."

She looked at him sadly. "You said that yesterday, love."

Tears pricked Ben's eyes. He felt he was
losing Grandpa Joe, losing the chance to get
answers to all those difficult questions, losing
the chance to heal this horrible feeling of
being split in half. Mum hugged him, but it
didn't make it better.

"I'll make pancakes for breakfast," she
said, "and you can put as much syrup on
them as you like."

Mum was trying to be kind. He would eat
the pancakes even though he was less hungry
than he'd ever felt. He didn't want to look in
the mesh cage. He couldn't bear to. But as
he finished getting dressed, the twins rushed
in for their morning look at the "butflies".

"Ben! Ben!" Beedee squealed. "Loook!"

"Mummy! Mummy!" Deebee yelled. "Quick, the butflies is being borned!"

The girls were right. Something was fluttering inside the cage. One of the butterflies had emerged and was gently beating its new wings to dry them. It was perfect.

For a moment, Ben was lost in wonder. He thought about those tiny, maggoty little caterpillars and how it hadn't felt possible that they could turn into something as beautiful as a butterfly. Now he *really* understood why Grandpa Joe had always been "butterfly bonkers".

Over the next hour Ben, with his mum and the twins, watched as, one after another, the chrysalises split open and the new-born butterflies crawled out.

They were a sorry sight to start with, their wings wet and crumpled.

"They look like I do when I get out of the shower!" Mum said.

"They don't sing as well as you, Mum." Ben laughed.

It was wonderful to see the butterflies stretch their wings and then to see the orange colour blush across their wings as they flapped and dried out.

"Can we have one on our hand?" Deebee asked.

"Yes, sweetie, you can," Mum said, "but not yet. There's a very important person who has to see them first."

*

Keith finished work early because of Easter, so they all drove over to Grandpa Joe's house, with Ben, the twins and the butterflies on the back seat. Mum had some chocolate brownies in a tin.

"Granny Lou's recipe," she said.

When they got there, Mum gave Ben her front-door key.

"You go in first!" she said. "We'll follow."

As always, Grandpa Joe was sitting on the sofa, in the blue glow of the TV screen.

"Hello, Grandpa Joe," Ben said.

Ben turned off the telly and pushed the bowl of half-eaten cereal out of the way so he could put the mesh cage of butterflies on the table. Joe put his head on one side as if he was listening to a very faint sound from far away.

Ben sat beside his grandfather. The butterflies were nothing special, Ben knew, but they were the kind that Grandpa Joe knew best and had loved all his life.

"Grandpa Joe," he said. "Look! I brought you some butterflies."

Ben held up the mesh cage in front of Grandpa Joe's face. Inside, the Painted Ladies danced around, and Ben watched as Joe began to see them, to watch them.

67

Something in his face changed, like a
light coming on in a dark house.

Very softly, Ben put his hand inside
the cage and caught just one butterfly. Its
delicate papery wings pushed against his
fingers.

"This one is really special. I reared it in
my room. It emerged this morning, specially
for you."

The butterfly had stopped struggling.
Softly, Ben put it on Grandpa Joe's hand. He
feared it would take off, but it sat happily,
fanning its wings, as if Grandpa Joe were a
favourite flower.

"Remember the butterflies in your garden, Grandpa?" Ben asked. "The butterfly safaris?"

For what seemed like a long time, Joe stared at the butterfly on his hand. At last

he spoke. His voice wasn't like the silent whisper of the ghost he had been these past months – he sounded like Grandpa Joe again.

"Painted Ladies," Grandpa Joe said. "They lay eggs on the nettles at the end of the garden. Small Tortoiseshells do too. And Peacocks. But the Painted Ladies were Stewart's favourite. I've got a photo of him with one sitting on the end of his nose."

Grandpa Joe looked up and Ben saw he was starting to cry.

"But you, Ben, you've never been so keen on the butterflies. Lou's baking, that was your thing."

"I do like them now, Grandpa Joe," Ben said. "Now I understand why you like them. I want you to teach me all about them."

Grandpa Joe looked into Ben's face as if he was seeing him for the very first time.

"Good," he said. "That's very good."

Then Grandpa turned to the cage.

"We should let these go!" he said.

"Yes," said Ben, "but I think the whole family should do that together."

Grandpa didn't get a chance to reply, because Deedee and Beedee had come into the room with their mum and dad. They

were all a bit shy and they didn't say much.
Mum bent to kiss Joe gently on the cheek.

"Hello!" said Grandpa. "And hello, girls.
Goodness me, you've grown like weeds."

"Good to see you, Joe!" Keith said. "It's
been too long."

"It has indeed," said Joe. "I haven't been
myself. Not since Stewart. Then Lou. Not
myself at all. I apologise."

"Nothing to be sorry for, Joe," Mum said.
"We're all here now, that's the main thing."

*

The sun in the garden was warm for the first time that spring. Grandpa Joe and Ben stood in the sunshine and opened the mesh cage together. The butterflies milled about in the

air for a moment but soon got down to what was important – feeding. There were plenty of flowers already in bloom for them.

"Wherever have I been, Ben?" Grandpa Joe asked.

"I'm not sure." Ben smiled. "But I'm glad you're back – that's what matters."

It was Mum's turn to cry now.

"I think we need some cake," she said with a sniff. "I brought chocolate brownies. But the back door's slammed shut and my keys are on the hall table."

"Oh, it's fine," said Grandpa Joe. "There's a spare key. Lou hid one in the wall by the dustbin."

"You knew all along!" Ben cried.

"I did!" said Grandpa Joe. "All along."

And suddenly they were all laughing as they went into the kitchen to eat cake.

CHAPTER 6

THE BUTTERFLY HOUSE

Mum and Keith sold their house too. It sold almost as fast as Grandpa's. Together with Grandpa Joe, Mum and Keith bought a new house. It wasn't much bigger than either of the old ones, but its garden was huge, with a dinky little bungalow, perfect for one, at the bottom.

Packing up and moving out of their old house was a huge job. Beedee and Deebee had so many toys, and Keith had loads of old computers.

Helping Grandpa Joe to move out was a doddle. It was still only lunch-time when the furniture van drove off down the road and Grandpa Joe locked his front door for the last time.

"You OK, Joe?" Mum said.

"Yes, I really am," Grandpa Joe replied. "But I think we need an outing now. How about that tropical butterfly place you told me about, girls? In the zoo."

"I thought you only liked British butterflies, Grandpa," said Ben.

"Well," Grandpa Joe said, "I'm allowed to change my mind, aren't I?"

"You certainly are." Mum smiled.

"Y'all have fun!" said Keith. "I have an errand to run. Catch you later!" and he gave Mum a look.

What now?! Ben thought.

*

Grandpa Joe was almost as excited as the girls about the visit to the tropical butterfly house. They each held one of his hands, and all three very nearly skipped in through the doors.

It was so hot and steamy inside that Mum's glasses misted up. Ben liked it a lot more than he'd expected. The big lush plants and the smell of things growing. But most of all the huge butterflies, especially the shiny blue ones gleaming in the shadows like giant jewels.

All around, bits of fruit had been put out for the butterflies to feed on, so you could get really close to them, and some of them even landed on your hands. Within minutes, Grandpa Joe and the twins had dozens walking up their arms.

"Their feets tickles!" Beedee told Joe.

"They're tasting you with their feet!"
Grandpa Joe told her.

"Is that true?" Deebee asked.

"It's true." Grandpa Joe smiled at her. "Cross my heart. Butterflies really do taste things with their feet!"

Afterwards they went for ice creams, and while they sat in the sun licking them, Keith walked up with a big parcel and an even bigger smile.

"Did I miss the fun?" he asked.

"Not at all." Mum laughed. "The fun starts when we get back home and have to start unpacking all the boxes in our new house!"

"Ah, yes!" said Grandpa Joe. "I can't say I'm looking forward to all the mess."

"I have a little something that may help you settle in, Joe," Keith said as he handed Grandpa the big parcel. "It's a present for your new house."

It was a sign that read "The Butterfly House", and it was decorated with perfectly drawn Painted Ladies!

"That's perfect!" Grandpa Joe said. "Perfect."

Keith drew another parcel out of his bag. "And here's the parcel you wanted me to pick up, Joe." Grandpa and Keith smiled at each other.

I don't believe it, thought Ben, *more grown-ups giving each other "looks"*.

Grandpa Joe turned to Ben. "This is for you. For your new room," he said. "It's from the three of us, really. I took the photo, but it needed a bit of digital cleaning up, which your mum did. And Keith got a frame for it."

Ben opened his present. It was a beautiful photo, really one of Grandpa Joe's best. It showed a boy, a bit like Ben, with untidy dark hair and deep-set blue eyes. He had a butterfly on the end of his nose. Its wings were bright orange, splashed with white and black, as if someone had used a paint brush to decorate it just a moment before. The smile the boy wore was sunshine itself, full of delight and mischief. Ben knew that he'd have liked that boy very much indeed.

"I'm going to tell you all about him,"
Grandpa Joe said, "when you visit me in my
new house. My butterfly house!"

Our books are tested
for children and young people by
children and young people.

Thanks to everyone who consulted on
a manuscript for their time and effort in
helping us to make our books better
for our readers.